Conte

Chapter One: The Faeries at The En(
Page 1

Chapter Two: The Arsonist of Slate Street
Page 9

Chapter Three: The Eels of Thawncliffe
Page 15

Chapter Four: Madame Hogsworth's Pretty Porcelain Dolls
Page 21

Chapter Five: How The Devil Left Hell
Page 25

Chapter Six: I Met The Devil in a Jazz Bar
Page 29

Chapter Seven: The Carousel of Fletcher Street
Page 33

Chapter Eight: The Figure by The Grandfather Clock
Page 41

Chapter Nine: Eden Lost
Page 49

Chapter Ten: Death And The Suicide
Page 55

Chapter Eleven: The Snowmen of St. Mary's Orphanage
Page 61

Chapter Twelve: The Comfort Of Our Lives
Page 65

Chapter Thirteen: The Cicada's Whisper
Page 73

For Vester, for always standing by my side.

For Fox

Happy Trans Pride!
—Petrichor

PETRICHOR MOSS
THE NOCTURNE'S FABLES

1

THE FAERIES AT THE END OF THE GARDEN

From Blackbush to Crownthorpe stretched my little kingdom. My childhood was still well in its precocious summer, and I? I was not yet eight, having turned seven just that winter. My friends were few and far between: Alvin lived in the cottage across the valley and over the hill, and Drew by the woods down the river.

Although it was rare that I would get the chance to see them outside of Saint Thomas' Primary School, I was never in lack of companionship. While the other children of the valley had dogs, cats, or even horses, while some made do with written companions such as Miss Shirley or Mr. Crusoe, I had the company of faeries.

Across the gravel driveway, past the sealed off well, to the left of the hortensia bush at the end of the garden, lay a fallen tree. A storm had blown down the great dark oak, some years ago, lifting its roots from out the earth, and sending the top of its branches through the window of my room.

Mother had shrieked at the miracle, while I had stood there, unscathed, in awe of the faeries' power. Every day since then, I would make my way to the foot of the tree, where the twisted and snapped roots revealed a great cavernous underground, and wish the faeries a pleasant day before setting off to school.

I cannot remember the first time I asked them for something. I think perhaps that I had been jealous of something or other, some backpack one of my cohort had brought. My own had never quite been new, even before it had been mine. A construction of black canvas and white thread, where my mother's inexpert stitching wove a fable of woe I had been too young to understand.

And so I wished. The backpack with an action hero on the front. A pair of left-handed scissors to fit my clumsy hands. A fountain pen that didn't leak ink over my lessons. And one by one, my prayers found themselves answered. I would return in the eve to those dark and shrunken roots, and there, placed before the entrance to the fey realm, would lie their gifts.

There were limits to the fey's power, even then. Once I had wished for a sports car, not out of any real desire, mostly out of a sense of childish curiosity, and had found myself rewarded with a matchbox car for my efforts. It had enjoyed a place upon my nightstand for many years.

I only felt the urge to share this power once. It was something the faeries did not seem to approve of. They were mine, after all. They had chosen me.

I often wondered why they had, out of everyone. Despite it all, I wasn't particularly unhappy. The objects of my desire were persistent, the gifts firmly appreciated, yet I couldn't shake the feeling that this power should go to someone else.

I had spent several nights awake, contemplating this, haunted by a memory the same way my friends were haunted by recurring nightmares. It had begun when the faeries first visited, when their realm had collided with my own. I'd awoken, thirsty one night, to my mother sitting at the kitchen table, well past suppertime, peering over a collection of papers stamped in red ink, and had watched her cry.

It's a strange experience, watching your mother cry. Never in my life had I felt so inept, so incapable than I did then, watching as she forced herself to pick up a red pen, and putting away her tears like papers in an envelope, continued on.

I had tried my best to comfort her, in the way that children know. I had listened to her stories when she felt inclined to read them, and ignored the clattering of the typewriter after she had set me to bed. It had worked, for a while, until the bad men came.

I think they had tried to come when I was still in school. Once enough years passed for my mother to be able to speak freely, she told me she suspected as much. There were certain things that most people, no matter how wicked they were, would not have a child bear witness to. This was one of them.

Wednesday had been a half-day. They must have forgotten that. The door was open as I returned, splintered where the guarding lock had been. Mother was sitting in the kitchen, her left cheek red. Above her, a man was shouting—a threat that sounded like words, but took the form of errant spittle. By his side, another leaned on a crowbar.

"Mom? What's going on?"

The words were calculated. Any child knows danger when he sees it. It's one of our greatest social myths—that the innocence of a child renders them dumb. Though the form may be alien, may evolve over time, no child is incapable of understanding violence.

The shouting man stopped mid-tirade. A red to match my mother's cheek rose to his face.

"These gentlemen just stopped by for tea." My mother answered, pulling me into a tight embrace. "And they were leaving."

The pointed stare is another thing adults believe children can't understand. A private, inaudible conversation for their eyes only. Yet I knew then exactly what that stare meant.

The bad men mumbled something I had not heard, wrapped in my mother's embrace, and left, the door shutting behind them.

"Go to your room." Mother had ordered. I had obeyed at once. While her tone had carried no suggestion of punishment, there was a finality to it I was not eager to test.

I'm ashamed to admit that that was the first time I asked for something for my mother. The following morning, before school, I asked for a knife. A sharp one. It was the only time the faeries did not offer anything at all.

Mother took to writing ever more readily. For months, sleep was kept at bay by the clacking of keys sounding until the ringing of the church bells announced the dawn.

The faeries had grown colder then, their gifts more sparse. I wondered if I'd done something to offend them, and even began returning some of their gifts, yet they always seemed to find their way back to my room by my return.

We moved too quickly for me to learn what I'd done to offend them. Mother's book had sold, and I was whisked away from Saint Thomas, from Blackbush and Crownthorpe, from all that I'd ever known without even a chance at a proper goodbye.

Mother had told me the news on Monday. We had left by Friday. In the hour before the moving van came, I had run off to say goodbye to the faerie kingdom, to ask if they were still mad at me, and had obtained no response. The moving van took all their gifts to our new house in the South of London, and we had followed suit.

There were no fallen trees in our new yard. A small cherry tree welcomed us, along with rose blooms, and I knew then that the fey had left me. I was not one for want, in our new home. My mother doted on me like no other, and gave me everything I wished for. A bike, for my eighth; a computer for my twelfth, a car for my sixteenth. Yet still, I missed my faeries.

I had written to them, once before my childhood had given way to adolescence, and addressed the letter to:

The Faeries At The End Of The Garden

55 Churchyard Way

Blackbush On Crownthorpe

UK 4FG23H

The response I received had been in cursive glitter ink. I threw it away.

My faeries would remain silent the rest of my life. Perhaps there comes a time when we are too old for such things, when we are left to face the brittle cold of adulthood alone, to learn to put away our desire for magic and wonder, and to file it under the fanciful memories of a childhood well lived. It is an injustice, and it is one we all must bear.

My mother died on the 13th of March 1989, and my faerie kingdom went with her.

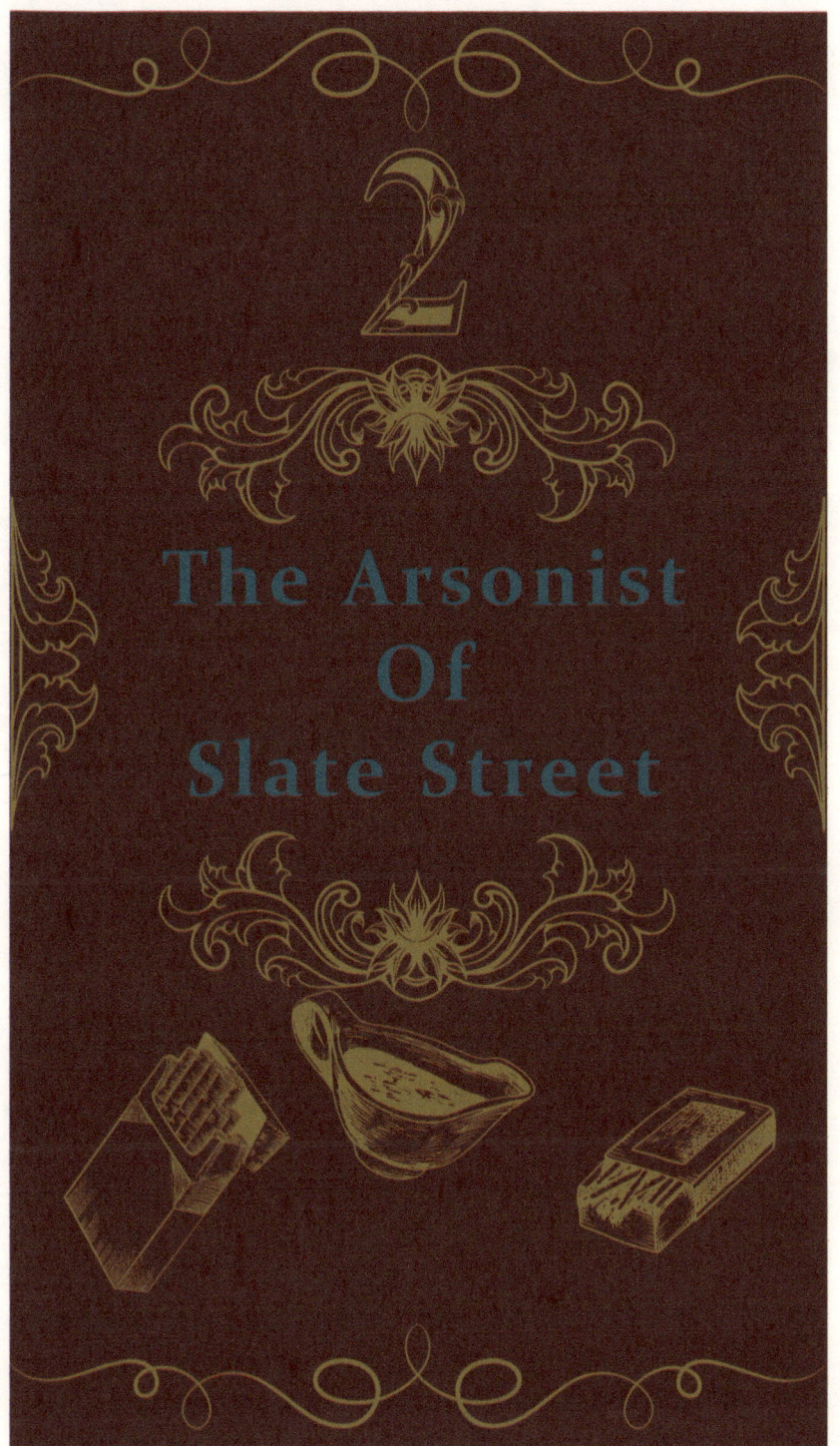

2
The Arsonist Of Slate Street

Adam wiped the sweat from his brow with the sleeve of his denim jacket. The still, SoCal summer air was sweltering, and the heat seeped into his flesh. Adam paused for a second, leaning against his battered Buick, scraping his calloused hands on the chipped brown enamel as he stared at the old house.

It had been Linda's idea. Adam had always wanted a log cabin by the woods, but Linda had insisted on a home in the suburbs—a great place to raise the kids, she said. She'd even found local Christian schools that would gear the children towards being "upstanding members" of society. Adam grunted.

It hadn't been her fault. No one had known about the asbestos. The house ended up having to be foreclosed and the bank refused to hear a word about it. Adam turned and got two cans of paint stripper out of the passenger seat.

He sighed again, and tread over the dry brown grass to the porch, where he sat on the rusted porch swing. The oak wood had gone gray as the rain water began to wash away the varnish, and the slats splintered under his weight. Adam reached into the pocket of his denim jacket and pulled out a pack of cigarettes.

The department called them "kill sticks", and he'd done his best to hide this vice from his colleagues. Cigarettes are not only a leading cause of cancer, but also of fires.

A surefire way to kill yourself, the department head had said. Adam had merely nodded.

He lit a cigarette, and getting up, took a key out of his pocket and unlocked the door. It's almost unbelievable what stress will do to a marriage. The hardwood floor had long swelled from the rain that seeped through the cracks in the slate roof, and he navigated places where the flooring had given out to rot. Adam placed the paint stripper by a pile of junk in the center of the living room.

It started with Linda having to get a second job. She'd gotten one, so Adam had to get one—never mind that he worked for a government service and always had to be available for most of the week. So he got a night shift flipping burgers with kids half his age. He'd swallowed his pride.

Then the kids' schooling gets more expensive to deal with budget cuts, so they have to go to public school—then one of them breaks their arm in a fight, and suddenly you're looking at thousands in unpaid medical bills. The cigarette sizzled in his hand, and Adam flicked it, sending ash upon a moldy carpet.

Suddenly you're taking out loans just to survive. Suddenly you're not as good a father as everyone thought you were. Suddenly every time your wife looks at you, you can hear the accusation in her eyes—the accusation that you aren't doing enough. The cigarette sizzled once more, and the heat began burning away at Adam's fingers as the cigarette burnt out. He dropped it onto the floor, watching as the embers slowly turned black.

Soon enough, the silent stares become words. Just comments, here and there. A few words of frustration. Some comments that were taken back almost immediately, but still the eyes continued to accuse in bitter silence. Adam traced a finger down the door frame.

Veins of asbestos ran through the fabric of this house, buried deep in every wall, just out of sight. The words became physical, after a time. Adam bent down and picked up a broken gravy boat from the pile of junk at his feet. Linda had picked it out herself from the registry. Her mother had bought it for them.

"We'd been happy, once, hadn't we?" He muttered. He obtained no response. A glint caught his eye, and he reached down and picked up a picture frame. The glass had cracked, but the old photograph still stuck to the frame. "You were smiling." Adam said.

It was a picture from their wedding. Linda's long blonde hair was done in long braids that were woven into her veil. Adam stood behind her, his eyes sparkling. "You're as beautiful as on our wedding day." Adam whispered. He tossed the porcelain and the picture frame onto the ground. Then he picked up the cans of paint stripper.

It had been Linda's idea. When Josh had left her, she said, the only thing she could do was burn everything that reminded her of him. "Fire cleanses. Fire illuminates," she said. She'd said as the fire had burnt; she realized she had never really loved Josh. She'd just loved the thrill of getting away with something.

It had taken a few days, but Adam had collected everything. It was fitting, he thought, to burn everything in this home. Where it had all gone wrong. The world would still turn, impervious to human correction, but we would know better—we would see the places in the tapestry where the fibers had run ragged and been replaced, by mortal artist's trembling hand—as a final act of spite.

Adam opened the cans of paint stripper and began pouring them out. A bucket of gasoline is suspicious. It raises questions. But anyone can buy as much paint stripper as they'd like.

Adam recoiled as the acrid smell hit his nostrils. He pulled out a pack of matches, and flipped it between his fingers, marveling at its weight. "We could have been happy. We could have made it work." He whispered.

Adam opened the matchbox, and pulling a match out, struck it. The sulfur hit his nostrils as the heat swept across his already sweating brow.

He looked up at the pile of trash, from the registry gifts to the photo albums, to the children's abandoned toys, into the eyes of the gagged woman, bound to a chair atop it all. The eyes that pleaded. That finally no longer accused.

"I love you," Adam whispered.

The match dropped.

Fire cleanses. Fire illuminates. The flames peeled back the pale drywall, and after a while, all that was left were the varicose asbestos veins.

3

THE EELS OF THAWNCLIFFE

Thawncliffe is a backwater and decrepit fishing town, built on the edge of a great chalk cliff that is forever tumbling into the sea. The weathered people who live there spend their days just as toughened leather—unyielding and difficult, they ignore their floundered potential that had long been drained away by the salty ocean air.

Thomas Earnshaw had been Thawncliffe's best and brightest, many a year ago. It was a pity then that as time went on, buffeted by the winds, Thomas' young optimism and drive began to—just like everything else in Thawncliffe—wither away into the sea.

Thomas watched as the murky salt claimed his father's lungs on an autumn night. The ocean, which had long been just a challenge on the way to distant shores he would someday visit, became his warden—and away, across the gulf, a dreamt-up shore plunged into the depths and began to rot on the ocean floor.

It's called a whale fall—a great beast of wonder sinks into the depths, and the fall from grace is enough to fuel ecosystems for decades.

Thomas' despair flourished in the long night of winter, and by the time the dawn broke at the equinox, his skin had grown mottled and jaundiced—as unyielding and as tough as leather. When the ice thawed off from the frozen waves and the sea began to roar once more, he boarded a ship of steel and pine, and drove his hands into the writhing depths.

Earl, the captain, recognized the madness that took his shipmate in tow in the way his hands gripped the bitter sea and his teeth bared against the cruel wind. Soon, Earl took Thomas under his wing, and the two became thick as thieves. Thomas' skin never recovered, but that was all the same to him.

Beside Earl and the waves of the pale gray sea, he dared allow himself to find something akin to peace. And although he stopped reaching through the waves in hopes of a spectral hand, he never left the ocean far behind.

Earl was the first to wed, and a couple of years later, Thomas joined him in tying the knot with Mary, a baker's daughter he did not love. Earl and Thomas started catching eels at low tide. They brought in enough to make a living.

It was at the end of their first week that Earl began the tale of Thawncliffe's eels. "Eels aren't really born", he said, "so much as made".

"You see kid, Thawncliffe has a way of getting into yer skin. And if it does for long enough, and if you let it happen, it'll change ye."

Thomas had merely nodded. Yet as their boots squelched in brown silt, he felt Thawncliffe creep just a little deeper inside his flesh.

Earl's wife passed a little while later from tuberculosis. Earl was convinced sea salt had taken to her lungs. "They just grow, in there. Rough little crystals growing like mangroves, until they tear you up from the inside." Thomas had just nodded, and together, they marched on into the autumn of their lives.

The sea had grown colder than they remembered in childhood, and the waves had lost whatever color they had once held. A field of gray mottled with dirty beige was laid out before them that morning, and the pair put on their boots, grabbed their instruments of hunting—here a net, there a club, and set off in search of their prey.

Behind them, Thawncliffe drew ever smaller, but refused to dissipate completely. It hung there, watching upon the cliff, as the pair trekked through the muddy debris of Thawncliffe's sunken dreams. Thomas pressed on, past what had once been a child's cot, cast-off into the currents to become nothing more than driftwood. There, a wedding veil floated on a wave's crest, lamenting a love that hadn't been true.

Thomas picked up the veil, staring at it for a moment before casting it into the bay. His jaundiced skin troubled him, and he adjusted his glove as he gripped the club tighter. Behind him, Thawncliffe twinkled.

"I know you're fucking my wife, Earl."

Earl started; his fingers clenched around a locket he'd found in the mud.

"What?"

"Don't lie to me."

Earl turned and stared. Thomas' black eyes stared back, scintillating against his spotted skin.

"So what if I am?" He said, after a moment had passed. "You don't love her anyway."

Thomas stared at the rocking surf. Before them, a piece of driftwood caught a wave, and headed out to sea.

"When I was a boy, I only wanted three things. I wanted a wife. I wanted a friend. And I wanted to leave." The stare of Thomas' dark eyes returned to Earl.

Earl swallowed. Thawncliffe was a dot above Thomas' shoulder.

"I'm sorry." He whispered, to his oldest friend.

Thomas did not come home that night. Fishermen would tell of a solitary figure trekking through the mud, casting off the clothes about his jaundiced and mottled skin, until—as easily and as effortlessly as he had jettisoned the rest of his dreams, he abandoned his humanity and slithered off into the depths.

4
MADAME HOGSWORTH'S PRETTY PORCELAIN DOLLS

Madame Hogsworth had always considered herself a good mother to her dolls. Back when she had been a younger woman, they had been the talk of all her friends. They were so pretty. So perfect. Their alabaster white skin unmarred by the sun's hot rays, their cheeks' red blush the only color allowed.

It wasn't long until the other girls came to her asking for advice on making their dolls pretty. Poor, pitiful girls brought along their broken little things. She helped them of course. It wasn't their fault they were bad mothers. Some girls just didn't care enough.

She sighed as she remembered the years gone by and the dolls that had come and gone—they'd become better, prettier. Madame Hogsworth made her way down the hallway, and unlocked the door at the end of the hall. She'd had a room made specifically for them. Only the best for her dolls. The door creaked as she opened it gently and made her way to the bed where she had last placed Melinda. She turned on the lamp on the bedside table. Its dim glow wouldn't mar Melinda's perfect porcelain skin.

Madame Hogsworth tutted as the light shone on Melinda's inert frame. The orange light cast shadows, but it wasn't enough to hide the cracks in Melinda's arm. "Foolish girl. What have you done now?" Madame Hogsworth scolded. She sat her doll against the headboard. "Now let's see what we can do, shall we?" Madame Hogsworth muttered. Melinda's blank blue eyes stared at her silently.

Madame Hogsworth's Pretty Porcelain Dolls

"Don't look at me like that." Madame Hogsworth snapped. "I'm very disappointed in you." Madame Hogsworth took a box from the nightstand, and took a brush out of it, dabbing it in the white powder. "This will mask your skin, and make you pretty again. There. Good as new."

Melinda's glassy eyes continued to stare blankly. "No. I already told you, you're too fragile to be taken outside." Melinda's lips were frozen in a blood-red pout. "There are people out there that don't want you to be pretty. There are people out there that will hurt you."

People were cruel. But Melinda was safe here. Madame Hogsworth grimaced. When she was a young girl, she'd been teased about her figure. Piggy Porker they'd called her. Piggy Porker, oink, oink! It had been too late for her, but she could still make her dolls beautiful. No one would ever hurt her dolls.

Madame Hogsworth shed a tear as she remembered her first dolls. They'd been... ugly little things. Ugly, spiteful things until she had... fixed them. She fixed them with her love. But when the other mothers saw, they were jealous. They were jealous of her dolls. They got boys to enter her home, and when they saw the shattered porcelain on the floor, they took her dolls. It didn't matter to them when she told them she was fixing them; that she was making them pretty so the world would like them. The boys in blue had taken her dolls to raise as their own. Madame Hogsworth was alone again. Ugly, in a cruel, unsightly world.

"Now you just rest and look pretty, dearie. Madame loves

you." She propped Melinda against the headboard once more. "And no more nonsense from you." Madame Hogsworth left and locked the door behind her.

The world had taken her dolls from her. It was cruel. She was only making them pretty. She deserved dolls, didn't she? She was a better mother than all the other girls who let their dolls grow into ghastly little things. They didn't deserve their dolls.

Tucked away in a dark room at the end of a long hallway, a single teardrop made its way out of Melinda's glassy eye as blood seeped out of the cuts in her skin.

HOW THE DEVIL LEFT HELL

At the turn of the century, The Devil had gotten himself stuck in a bit of a rut. The... debate on the nature of men's souls remained unanswered as of yet—as the final reckoning was to be had at a much later date, yet the trickle of damned souls into the infernal caverns had begun to slow.

Concerned that his demonic legion wasn't doing enough to tempt the mortals into sin and the wallowing of the flesh in empty pleasures, he decided to journey upwards to the green pastures of Earth. Green is a color that is lacking in hell, amidst the reds and yellows of infernal fire and brimstone, but it is the green of envy that tints mortal souls and leads them astray, and it would be green that would tempt the Devil himself.

Her name was Amelia, and her eyes were as green as Eden. It had been pure circumstance. Mr. Thomas Roberts had always considered himself a gambling man, and it was amidst a game of poker that the Devil made his acquaintance. Mr. Thomas had little clue as to the nature of his guest, yet the bids slowly became more and more absurd—the Devil promised him wealth beyond his wildest dreams, and Mr. Roberts watched in shock as the Devil delivered on bid after bid.

The Devil knew Mr. Roberts had been had—a flicker of recognition had struck his face, breaking his practiced steely facade before he smiled—asking his partner for everlasting glory. The Devil acquiesced and was about to demand his eternal soul if he lost—when he laid his eyes on hers. Amelia had stared at him curiously from across the room, drawn by some form of magnetism—a heat within the Devil she had mistaken for warmth.

And so the Devil asked for her hand. And Mr. Roberts acquiesced. And the Devil won—twice. Mr. Roberts would go on to offer his soul in a later game, and sealed his fate. Amelia and the Devil began to court each other, falling head over heels—and so the Devil neglected his duties in Hell, for a life in New Orleans.

But it was not to be. Amelia had remained... unaware of the particularities of her new lover, and the Devil, in his shame, sought to hide it from her. But alas, the Devil is not welcome on consecrated ground—a detail he had missed in his urge to wed his beloved, and so his mortal form burst into flames as he crossed the threshold of the church, and the truth was revealed to his wife-to-be.

She had fled as the Devil did his best to cover his face and horns, amidst the shocked parishioners—she ran and didn't stop running until she had reached a convent and taken her vows: so that she may be cleansed of the Devil's sin.

The Devil returned to Hell, where he was greeted with a warm welcome. The demons had longed for the guidance of their lord, yet the Devil was in no mood for state affairs. He locked himself in his chambers as the years passed on, and the demons soon grew accustomed to his plaintive cries joining the lament of all Hell's sinners.

Amelia was claimed by Heaven twenty years later, and the Devil lost her forever. In the midst of his grief, the demons brought him a visitor.

There is one man in the whole of Hell who shall not be touched. Who amidst the cries of the damned and the laughter of the sane, ringing out until the final judgment, plays Baccarat and reminisces on his life long past. The Devil visits him no longer. It was his eyes—his eyes of green, that drove him to leave.

6
I MET THE DEVIL IN A JAZZ BAR

When I was 19, I met the devil in a Jazz bar in New Orleans. It was a swing bar, and when I say swing... well, you know. New Orleans is a bustling, chaotic place, especially on Mardi Gras, but looking back I'd have sooner traded my bead necklace for a rosary. I'd made my way through a crowd of people in various states of inebriation and nudity and had found myself in front of a speakeasy—my brother Tom had recommended the place, and I was more than eager to drown my sorrows in cheap liquor and the blues.

Edelweiss, the password was. The almost mystical flower that grows on Northern slopes in Western Europe. You can spend your whole life looking and never find it. It's a shame isn't it—something so coveted being so far out of reach for many. But after all, that's why we covet, isn't it? It separates those with willpower—those who'll do anything it takes... from those who won't.

I sat at the bar, swirling a vintage in a rocks glass to the sound of the live band. The sax player was demiurgic, and the melody rang out, flowing like the liquor that was all too readily imbibed. And that's when he sat beside me. I wish I could say he was hideous with horns and fangs, or as handsome as they come with all the false veneer of charm you could muster from the Lord of Lies and Seduction, yet I cannot remember what he looked like. He was as plain as they come, wearing a dull green tweed jacket, worn with age.

He sat next to me and said, "Son, the true measure of a man is in brass and liquor," and I agreed. "Tell me, son," he said, "what compels you so to drink your sorrows away?" To which I replied, "Sir, I sought fame and fortune as an entertainer, but I was usurped by another." The Devil sighed, and drank his liquor. "I know that all too well," he said to me.

The liquor had gone to my head and I found myself sharing more than I had wished to. He sat and listened, and didn't say a word the entire time—he just drank his bourbon and stared deep into my soul. He had a piercing gaze, yet I do not remember the shade of his eyes—just his intense gaze as I spoke about my ails.

"Son," he said, interrupting me, "you have my compassion. Yet you are not helpless—and clearly, you covet the role. And I know a thing or two about coveting."

"Son," he said, "the other man does not desire that which he has, and as such, he does not deserve it." He peered past my eyes once more, and I looked away. The upbeat sax had begun to bale a mournful tune.

"Son," he whispered into my ear, "how badly do you want this?" he asked—his eyes gazing at my soul. "Badly," I said. "I'd do anything." He continued to gaze with eyes more compassionate than I'd ever known—eyes I'd have mistaken for the Madonna's herself as he spoke:

"I have a gift for you, son." He said, pulling out a package from his tweed jacket. I took it with trembling hands, undid the twine and paper, and pulled out an ornate brass blade. "It's yours," he said. "To do with as you wish." He winked, and left the bar. Yet I know he awaits me, because I got the job.

I got the job because I desired it more. I did what it took. I won't pretend otherwise. I plunged the knife later that evening into that poor bastard's throat, and I knew then as I'm telling you now—the Devil doesn't make deals. He finds out what the truly desperate want, and makes them damn themselves—all the way down to Hell.

7
THE CAROUSEL OF FLETCHER STREET

My father was an engineer. At least that's what he would tell you as he tinkered on in the yard, much to the annoyance and dissatisfaction of my mother. The truth was he was an accountant enmired in a passionate love affair with wood and steel.

There was something in his eyes when he worked—a satisfaction found amidst screws and nails that nothing else could ever hope to provide—not even us, his son and his wife. Father found mistakes for a living. He fixed them as a passion.

And what a passion it was. The remnants of a Ford engine littered our kitchen, seeping its brackish black oil into the sink, beneath which was a moonshine still my father had acquired in an estate sale.

The yard housed a new project each week, and every Monday I would return to hold wrenches or hammers or whatever tool my father had decided on using that day. We spent every Monday working, my father and I. Every Monday, Mother left the house in a huff, clutching her purse to her chest.

It had been excitement. It had been adventure. As my father once put it: "It had been the days of wonder." Yet as my boyhood stumbled and fell away in the aftermath of adolescence, a question burned away at the back of my throat, clawing its way to the forefront of my tongue, slipping past my gritted teeth and through my pursed lips.

Father had been disassembling a Volkswagen when I'd asked: "Dad? How do we afford all this?"

A sourness had taken him at once, and he'd sent me to the store to fetch a left-handed screwdriver. From then on, every Monday was for him.

I was sixteen when Riley transferred over from Tennyson East. It was a Monday. He offered me a cigarette. I accepted. We traded stories in stuttering starts and stops. Riley was a "foster fuckup". Car crash. Lone survivor. 13 homes. 13 families. Some worse than others.

Riley was a driftwood bonfire—a pieced-together crackling scintillating on unstable shores, howling in the wind, and I loved him for it. Classes slipped away as we spent Mondays together, fingers tracing over hollow chests as our quivering voices hung in the air like cigarette smoke, set adrift in the heat.

I returned every nightfall to debris in the yard. Mother had already left by then, unable to stand it. Most days my father wouldn't even look at me. I got my first F. Spanish. I'd missed most classes that semester during my trysts with Riley. I stuck it to the fridge. My father had just stared at it, face full of disappointment, before grabbing a beer and returning to the yard.

"Congratulations," Riley had said, when I told him about it. "You're a foster fuckup. Just like me." We stopped going to classes altogether.

The yard became encapsulated in a steel dome over the next few months. I barely even noticed. The screeching of power tools had bled past its usual hours and now carried on from dusk till dawn. I had long lost my curiosity about my father's new projects, but this one was insurmountable in scale. To this day I still do not know how he got the building permits—if he even got the building permits.

We entered an unspoken agreement, my father and I. I would respect his privacy, and in return, he would respect mine. Neither of us spoke in anything other than grunts. It's impressive what you can say to each other without words.

I did find out what he was building, eventually. I'd been suspended after a fight, and had needed him to sign some form of acknowledgement. I could have forged the signature. I don't know why I didn't. Perhaps I'd done it out of spite. I'd turned the handle on the door to the great steel dome in our backyard, and had found myself in front of a carousel.

White sheets hung off the cresting. Cranking rods left exposed glittered with slick silver paint amidst banisters of gold and blue. Wooden horses lay off to the side, discarded. The central gear connected to a series of torque converters spiraling off in increasingly more complex mandalas about a central collection of figures, covered with a pale white sheet like little costume ghosts.

I'd pulled off the sheet to reveal my father's handiwork. Polished brass and wood revealed themselves to the halogen lights: automatons with two sets of faces, my mother's and mine. The flywheel spun with the flick of a switch, and I watched as the not-me whirred to life, a facsimile of everything I should have been.

I turned on my heels and left, walking past the foyer, past the gate, past the end of the road until finally I was at Riley's, and I had no idea how I had gotten there, but my face was bruised and my arm was cut and I had no idea how that had gotten there, but there were broken gears and shrapnel in my bag and I had no idea how they had gotten there, but the cops were speaking, asking if my father had done this to me, and I had no idea how they had gotten there, but there was a bandage on my wrist and Riley's arms were around me, and I had no idea how they had gotten there, and suddenly the fact that my father had struck me was in my file, but I don't remember how it had gotten there, and suddenly I was living with Riley—and I had no idea how I had gotten there.

I came back home only once more.

I'd managed to graduate, largely thanks to an unscrupulous senior who had sold me his essays. My father was not present. Riley, however, was. Later as we walked back from a celebration that had been entirely too much, he'd knelt to the ground, taken my hand in his, and asked.

We were going to trade school together—carpentry. Something my father might, at one point, have been proud of. Riley had driven me to the old house at my insistence, that I may retrieve some paperwork, and say goodbye to the place. My father still haunted the yard—a poltergeist that frightened the local children, screeching the haunted cries of tortured steel as he scattered debris about the neighborhood.

Riley had parked in the driveway, and left the engine idling as I entered the old home. The spare key was still under the mat. My bedroom was as I had left it. Model of the lunar lander still on the desk, amidst old homework I had never turned in. Comics lining shelves I'd put up myself as a child. Nothing had changed but I, yet somehow in the interim the space had grown too small for anyone to live in.

I found my birth certificate in my father's old safe. The combination had not been changed. I remember staring at the ink on the page, wondering how something so ordinary could be so important, before sighing and thrusting it into my bag.

I made it all the way to the foyer. All the way to the doorknob. All the way to the welcome mat. I could not move forwards despite myself. A rage kept me frozen in place, like a scream that buries itself in one's throat. Riley had stared at me with concern as I'd backed away and returned to the house. To the yard. To the steel dome my father had built to hide his shame. The screwdriver in my hand had been debris just moments before.

My father was in the carousel. Its ring gear was spinning, sending the contraption about himself in a perfect facsimile of domestic life—each action, each response, scripted, adjusted, made perfect through the madness of a man who would not deign even to look at us, except through mechanically manifested memories of a yesteryear that did not exist.

"I didn't hit you."

The man who had once been my father was now sat at a table in the center of the carousel, drinking from a bottle of Southern Comfort as the automatons scurried around him. He had heard me come in, but hadn't cared to turn around.

"I know."

"Then why did you tell them I did?"

"Would you rather I had tried to explain this?"

Another round of Southern Comfort was swirled in a rocks glass as he contemplated.

"It ruined my life." He said, watching the automatons embrace. A facsimile of love.

"You ruined mine."

He fell silent at that, as we both watched the carousel turn endlessly upon itself. I approached the table, and we sat together for the first time in years.

Before us, not-me was rushing off to school.

"I don't know how to fix this." My father whispered.

"I know." I responded, setting the screwdriver upon the table and sliding it over to him. "But you will. You're an engineer."

8
The Figure By The Grandfather Clock

There was a house that lies between the depths of memory and the water swept banks of the river Loire, there where the children used to roam, in search of toads sun-basking between river stones.

The house was an aged affair, and time has not been kind to her. Here, the oak boiseries have been pulled off walls, there plaster carved through her mosaic floors. Mice and vermin slunk away through holes gnawed through floorboards, and cobwebs dot the rooms like a piecemeal veil—the last vanity that was yet afforded to her. When her previous stewards had left, her caretakers for many generations, they had taken everything with them.

The manor was named Misty, after the way the morning fog enveloped it—a gray silk robe about the shoulders of a countess, in the hours before her ladies in waiting had awoken. The French farmers on the steep impasse beside her called the morning fog "brume", vernacular that evoked the way their furrowed brow formed ridges and valleys in silent contemplation of the new tenants.

They were a queer folk from the city. Bankers. They were strikingly aloof—in that proper city sort of way. They were as quiet and poised as their neighbors were boisterous and loud—dressed in suits and cashmeres at the turn of winter.

As they sat together in the evening, in the dining hall of their limestone fortress, tales of their misfortunes inevitably ran aground upon the pale exterior walls, and no trace of them ever disturbed their lips, or indeed the ears of their company.

This was in the days when their eldest was still yet a boy craving wilderness and adventure, a desire that was fulfilled with the little gang of rogues from a few houses down. Sometimes they were knights of a long-forgotten kingdom, fighting for the honor of their valiant king. Other times they were soldiers of the Great War, fighting their way across the orchards and vineyards of the French countryside.

Juvenile daydreams and fancies wove themselves into that place that was not quite fiction, and not quite fact. Tell me it wasn't true, that for a few hours they really had been Lancelot and Percival, searching for the grail! Oh, how King Arthur (the bankers' boy), and Lancelot (Jacques from down the lane) had held Percival (Martin from across the woods) in his dying breath and wept actual warm tears at the death of their comrade!

Still—daydreams erode in the night, when each playmate is forced to bid to each other "A plus, on se voit demain?" as they go their separate ways and join their families for dinner. The boy would always sigh as he stepped through the great green gates, over the overgrowth of ivies and nettles haphazardly kept at bay by gravel strewn upon the paths, towards a dinner in silence.

He never really told me quite when the nightmares started. Perhaps they were always there, looming somewhere

The Figure By The Grandfather Clock

below the surface, like great jagged rocks lurking underwater in wait of a ship's hull.

The boy awakens, nearly every night—heart racing, and parched for a glass of water. He reaches for the bedside table, beset with not one, but two lamps—and to his dismay, neither turns on. Outside, in the dark night, a lightless thunder rages. His bedroom door is ajar, though he has not left it so. It is an odd thing, but he ignores it, and the hinge squeaks as he opens the door and steps into the narrow hallway.

The dining room to his right is empty—though places are set for yet another silent meal. The hallway and dining room switches respond with a dull click to the boy's trembling fingers, as they too refuse to turn on.

It is dark, so very dark—and the child is afraid.

The kitchen sink hisses as the child opens the tap—but nothing comes out but air. A creak from the attic draws attention, and the child calls out to his parents—but the cry elicits no response. The door to their room is ajar as well—though it wasn't last night—and both their beds are empty.

The child is drawn by a ticking—the only sound in the house—as the thunder draws nearer. The spiral staircase descends into the depths, and it is all he can do to follow it, and the sound below.

The foyer is shuttered closed, and no light peers through the windows. The room is empty—apart from the grand piano, the ticking grandfather clock, and the figure that stands be-

fore it. It steps towards the child, and the child screams—yet nothing leaves his throat but a whimper.

"There is a leper," the boy said, "within the halls of this house." Jacques and Martin look amused, but listen intently as he continues. "His hands and his feet are stumps, and his skin sloughs off the bone. He has a wicked laugh and he chases, hobbling, after you."

"What does he want?" Martin asked, fingers trembling.

"Why isn't it obvious?" The boy answered with a smile. "He wants to take your flesh as his!" The boy cried, as he launched an attack upon his friend that left the two of them giggling and fighting for air.

That day the leper became cemented within their childhood games—the persistent, unrelenting villain that pursued them across aeons and genres, hidden and waiting to strike. Often, the troupe would slay him, but he would inevitably rise again, like Christ on Easter, and continue his pursuit.

And at night, when all the friends would part ways once more, the boy would walk past the great green gates, step into the foyer, and meet with the leper alone.

Martin was the first to leave for a prépa in Nantes. Jacques followed him a year later. The boy languished, alone in the manor for a number of years. They encountered each other once more—just once—in a tavern in Neuilly-sur-Seine. Jacques and Martin smiled as they reunited with their old friend.

The years have not been kind to him. He sported a hirsute beard—a patchwork of thin hairs his cheap razor had failed to cut through—and bandages around his wrist, where his razor had stayed true. He sat at the bar, drinking cheap Cognac straight from the bottle—ignoring the rocks glass that had been set before him.

Jacques and Martin ignored the bandages with the practised inexperience of proper gentlemen, as Martin served himself cognac from the bottle without returning it. Their friend's face yielded slowly to their jokes, and a smile cracked on his face, in the same way leather wrinkles when it's broken.

"What was that game we used to play?" Martin asked suddenly.

"Hide And Seek—with the Leper of Misty!" Jacques responded, with great raucous laughter. "How on Earth did you come up with it?" He asks.

The smile on their friend's face evaporates like a handprint on glass, and he stares at his drink before answering with a whisper. "The leper was real." He replied, and an involuntary shudder traces down his spine as he is taken by the memory of the leper's skin against his.

The hair upon his nape stands on end, in memory of the caressing breath that had once settled there. He shakes as the lips he sought so desperately to numb betray him with

The Figure By The Grandfather Clock

a phantom sensation, and haunted, reaches for the liquor.

Martin does not stop him this time. The two friends stare at their whimpering friend in a silence that will last forever. The friends will never write again. How could they? In every tear and inked stained letter Martin and Jacques will sit down to write, they will hate themselves for never having seen it—never, in all of their days—having seen the leering figure by the grandfather clock.

It is a secret that their friend takes to the grave. There was a new version of the dream—where the ending of the nightmare changed.

The lights stubbornly refused to turn on. That much was the same. And the thirst—the thirst did not change. The dining room is set for another silent meal, the kitchen tap only hisses and does nothing to quench his thirst. His parents' rooms are empty.

All was the same, except this: when he descended down the spiral staircase, fuelled on by the ticking of the grandfather clock, there was nothing there to meet him. No leper hissing with rotten breath just how badly he wishes to partake of his flesh, no shambling, clumsy pursuit as the boy tries in vain to flee.

The foyer was completely empty, apart from the grand piano and the grandfather clock, and drawn in by a shudder that settles in the spot just between his shoulder blades—the spot that is only warmed by liquor—he reached for the shutters on the windows, undoing the latch and throwing them open.

The town outside is dark and quiet. No street lights are illuminated. The houses down the impasse stand stoic—doors closed and lights off. The whole world is silent, apart from the lightless thunder and the ticking of the grandfather clock.

The silence is the knife that slips between his shoulders and twists between his ribs without so much as a whisper. It is the silence that reveals the true extent of the leper's curse.

There in the foyer, he sank to his knees, shattered beyond repair, and never rose again.

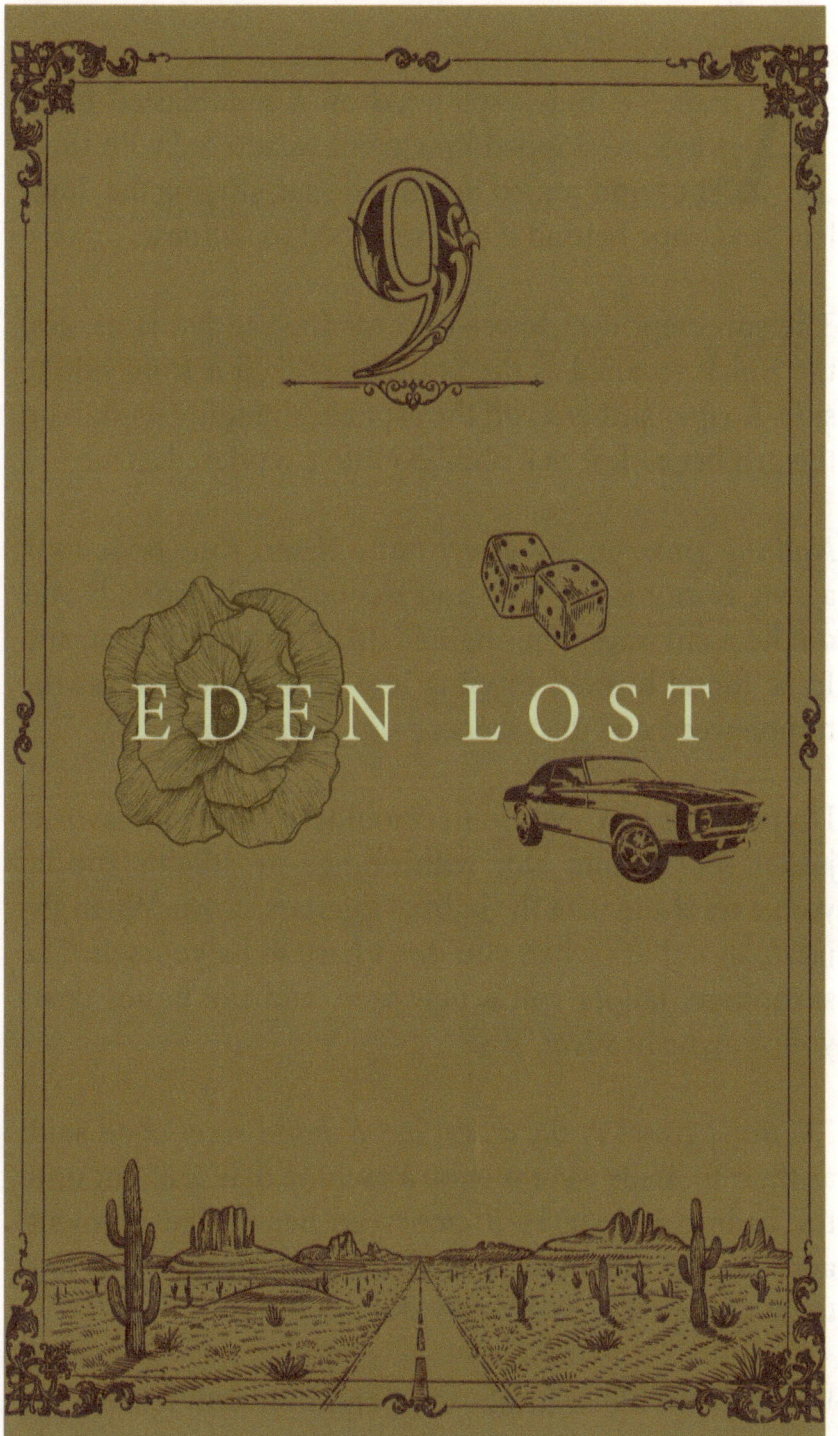

A battered Buick spattered on a sandblasted highway; the chipped lime paint weathered with time. The wind trailed behind the car, stirring the desolate landscape behind it as it returned to stillness.

The sun crept ever lower towards the sandy plains, and the Buick groaned as the potholes rocked it from side to side. A viper slithered off the asphalt, shedding its skin on the grit beneath it as it climbed into a withered shrub.

Nothing grows in the desert but a desert rose. Isaac took a swig from his hip flask and stepped on it. Nobody was out here anyways. The engine rattled up a drum beat, and Isaac found himself slipping into an old memory as the tumbleweed and dust scenery slipped past him.

Drape the night over your shoulders like your favorite jacket. Comb your hair with orange streetlights and let your eyes shine with the light of the stars above. When the jazz plays, that's when you don't have to be yourself. The saxophone tailors you a new face, and the liquor coats your tongue in silver.

"Nothing grows in the desert but a desert rose." she'd said; as their footfalls were met by a melody that spilt out onto the ballroom floor. He'd embraced her in that moment, and the night had swept them away for the dawn to find them wrapped in each other still.

We all begin life as bright-eyed children with faith in the

magicks of the world—before the sand erodes us. Faith is a specter of innocence lost, a fearful haunt of those who crave wonderment from this God-forgotten world. A small reprieve from stars until dusk—Ateh, Malkuth... Le Olahm, Amen.

Sit down child, and close your eyes. Imagine the longest stretch of time that feels real, and the most important thing you can do in that time. Push past to the times and places that are hidden. To times and places where the question doesn't make sense. Find where the half-forgotten daydreams feel dreamt up by another—where usurped desperate desires give way to blighted open plains. Where days and weeks find themselves scattered on a highway bridge, blowing in the wind as a spectral hand grips an ice-cold rail. A place where time floats beside an isolated figure, writing and rewriting a singular question.

The best he could have asked for and this is where it ends. An ice-cold whisper trembles down his sides. The bitter taste in his mouth rises to meet the lump in his throat. His voice coalesces into a spirit taking hold of his will, releasing him finger by finger.

And as he gazes into her almond eyes, she warns him. *"Nothing grows in the desert but a desert rose."* she says, lighting a cigarette. But he kisses her anyways, parting lips marred with cocaine and Xanax for a taste of tenderness. And the porcelain shatters on a shard of gypsum.

Fingers trace tender flesh under Selene's silver satin, rushing now, as the embers smolder in his gray eyes. Desire's yoke binds them together as the wayward shepherd leads them to slaughter.

Red wine stains white meat on eve of November's end. Tensions rise around a carcass in the hopes of withering budding love. Blood may be thicker than water, but wine flows more readily than both. And as the Romans say: "In vino veritas." Isaac hasn't been back since.

They take flight now and feel the City of Lights' rays beneath their wings. Gambling a life away on 21, drinking SoCal wine to the sound of slots and craps. Nothing's real out here, but both of them know: hidden amidst the porcelain tapestry lies the artist's hands.

A mystic's tent rises by nightfall, and within the old crone is draped in Tyrian purple. "Fifteen. The Devil." She whispers hoarsely, grimacing as the card comes up. "Here, six, The Lovers." The couple smirks. "Sixteen. The Tower." She picks up the card, and the couple laugh, but at the bottom of the deck lies Twelve, and in her mind the smiling man already hangs.

A night of mischief for the City of Sin. A pilgrimage of young men come to seek Fortune's favor in sacrifices of silver and gold. But as the wheel turns, hands sweep away scarlet serpents—as the mendicants leave in shame.

"*To love and to cherish until death do us part.*" The engine sputtered and gave out as the tank ran empty. The sun had just fallen behind the horizon and the azure night set a wave of indigo sand upon the desert. Isaac turned the windows down and prepared for the night.

There's truth, you know, in Pygmalion and Galatea. All warlocks seek to transmute stone into flesh—as Eliott writes: "Lips that would kiss form prayers to broken stone." We have all yearned to know marble that would not reward our trembling hand with Stygian cold. But at the very least, marble does not lie. *Sine cera, amans mei.* Isaac pulled a jacket over himself, and in the warmth of the desert night, he slept.

A man came around morning, and they shared a beer as the sun chased the night away. He gave Isaac gas, and they parted ways. The engine turned over, and after a brief pause, so did the wheels—and the car headed on its path once more.

"*To love and to cherish, until death do us part? ... I do.*" A night of inebriation ends in a dress of white silk. And so, by night's end, they found themselves betrothed as the knot was tied by a dead king. Bound together by twilight, the serpents writhed between satin sheets.

As the moon fell from the night sky, she recounted how Adam tasted Eve's forbidden fruit, and both left Eden like Lilith before them. Abandoned, Eden withered—*nothing grows in the desert but a desert rose*. She'd kissed him tenderly as the Sandman led him away, and by sunrise, she was gone.

Run away to New Orleans. Dance your nights away and drink away your mornings. Neat scotch for the taste of last night's cigarette—and for today's ecstasy. The witch sells voodoo but he knows better—black magick impregns this dance floor—he can taste it on his tongue, in the memory of her lips on his, in the numbness of his senses, in the touch of her—*Adonai Elohim, why have you forsaken me?*

The sax distorts in his drugged mind into a hymn for Lucifer. He invoked him, and so The Tempter beckoned, as the fallen prowled beneath the highway bridge. Faith is a specter of innocence lost—of a past life that now haunts in undeath. And Isaac leapt.

Salvation didn't happen between pews and stained glass. The white lights that greeted him weren't angelic, but fluorescent. Asclepius' wards would tend to him, not the saints. He'd been forsaken long ago. The prodigal son—lost and dreaming of home.

The prodigal son—wrapped in sheepskin and sent on his way.

It's a strange thing to live without love and light—to walk only the dark valleys of shadows where men go to die—a field where nothing grows. "And there was no more death nor pain, for the old world had slipped away overnight, and all that remained was dust." Because *nothing grows in the desert but a desert rose*, and you'll cut yourself to know those lips.

DEATH AND THE SUICIDE

Jeffrey was a suicide in progress. Whereas most have an experience of death as something quite abstract, as a matter for grammatical tenses, as a series of affairs wherein someone who once *was* suddenly *isn't*, to be carted away in a box of varnished wood, never to be seen again; Jeffrey had a much more intimate relationship with death.

See, it had all started when Grandfather Archibald croaked. He had the misfortune of breathing his last on a sweltering August morning, not one week into the coroner's honeymoon. And so, not long after he'd shuffled off this mortal coil did his remainder have to be moved to the attic, much to the revelry of the various house flies and spiders crawling about in the rafters.

Jeffrey had climbed up there once, and stood, watching as the body bloated, as if to fill the emptiness left behind. It was then that he understood: *All things are dirt struggling with meaning. One day the dirt wins.*

It was a sentiment he'd echoed to a girl he'd once loved:

"There will come a time when you will no longer hold any meaning. This is truth. This is the only truth. On that day, you will become dirt, and I will not grieve, I will not cry. I will dispose of you as one does with dirt, and carry on with my life."

It was one of the many reasons she left him. And when she

did, standing in the doorway with her suitcase, begging him to answer some question he did not remember, he'd said:

"Today the dirt won."

Salt and water had hit the ground, and Jeff wondered who would clean it now that she was gone.

The Buddhists have this thing called devotion to rite and ritual, which is just a fancy way of saying that sometimes people get too attached to the act itself, rather than the purpose. Jeff had thought then, as he did now, that surely this would extend to objects, or even to people.

Perhaps a person can become a kind of living dead, devoid of owner or purpose, a physicality with no meaning. Just a shambling collection of acts and rituals, held together with veins like twine, bound about some hollow core. The only case in which the dirt will not quite have won, at least not in the strictly material sense.

Perhaps, just as an orchid in dry soil, meaning too, can wither and die; and all that will be left is dust tumbling in an hourglass, counting down the minutes, with no ability to wonder why. Maybe that meaning is lost forever. Perhaps Death, in his kindness, seeks to preserve it.

There is a place where meaning goes, the day the dirt wins. Where all meaning will one day go. Jeff had seen it that day he'd snuck into the attic and watched his Grandfather's broken form.

Watching the dust tumble on the face of someone who both was and now isn't his grandfather, he found himself surprised by a tall figure in dark robes. The sickle in his hand shone as he brought it to Archibald's neck, and sliced. The figure whispered softly to the wound, and out came a timid and frightened creature, which crept into his hand. His hand slipped into the pocket of his robes, and with that, retreated to the shadows.

Death had taken his Grandfather into his robes, into the place where we will all one day go. Jeffrey had sat there, in awe, just beginning to comprehend what he had seen.

Jeffrey took to breaking things. Vases, precious to his mother. A television, precious to his father. Everything and anything he could. And each time, the figure appeared with his sickle, and reaped the purpose from the dirt. The figure never answered any questions, or indeed gave any indication that Jeffrey was there.

That is, until the day he turned sixteen. His father had paid handsomely for a used car, a pretty little thing of baby blue and just 3000 miles. Jeffrey took it out for a test run, and drove it into a tree. His father had decided then that he did not have anything left to say to him. It was the most valuable thing he had ever broken.

Death had come, in his tall dark robes, to reap what was sown. And the words had left Jeffrey's lips before the meaning had slid into the depths of his pockets—"Take me with you."

Death And The Suicide

Death had turned to him, and stared. Then, with a calm, light voice, had answered: "No."

Jeff had sat there, by the wreck, watching as Death receded into the shadows. Inside him, whatever meaning was left withered up and died.

Jeff would tell you that that was the day he passed. Tying the noose was just a formality. And so here he was, dotting the i's and crossing the t's, three years later. Three years later, and not one memory to call his own. He set the twine necktie over his shoulders, and prepared to drop.

Death's clear voice chimed as the stool wobbled: **"What do you think you are doing?"**

"What does it look like I'm doing?"

"Are you trying to force my hand?"

"I suppose so."

"It's not the way things work."

"I don't care."

The plunge into eternity stared out from Death's sunken eyes. The sigh of a thousand souls left his lips.

"You have no meaning for me to reap," he confessed.

The words hung in the air, on miniature nooses of their

own. Death raised his scythe to the rope, and reaped the liberation from it. Jeff clattered to the ground.

"Go. Live a life of meaning. Fill yourself with it."

And with that he returned to the shadows.

Jeffrey had stood there a long time, contemplating, but in the end, he lifted himself up, and with a long and heavy sigh, walked across the foyer, and opened the door to an overcast sky.

11
THE SNOWMEN OF ST. MARY'S ORPHANAGE

Mary crept out of bed, slipping on her frayed bunny slippers, and snuck past Mother Superior's room. She shivered as she clutched her light cotton cardigan. It was a cold winter, and the freezing draft nipped at her ankles like an insistent yipping dog. She made her way down the stairs, gently, trying to stop the stairs from creaking. She needed not worry, anyways. She was too light for that to be of any concern.

Mary turned the lock on the heavy oak door. The deadbolt clicked back with a dull thud. She held her breath. Silence. No one had heard. Truth be told, the nuns were rather liberal on the barbiturates. Not that Mary had any idea what a barbiturate was. As far as she was concerned, the sisters were just always tired and sleepy. They looked after a lot of orphans, after all. And not all of them were as well behaved as Mary. Mary grimaced as she thought about how Mother Superior would react to catching her out of bed, but she shrugged it off. She was doing a good thing, after all.

The other orphans said there wouldn't be Christmas this year, either. Santa Claus hadn't stopped by in a couple of years. Mother Superior said he must have missed the orphanage, amidst all the other good children. Not that they weren't good, she was always quick to add. Just that there were a lot of other children, and people just kind of... forgot.

So Mary would do her best, then. She'd make sure Santa

came this year. Then at Christmas mass tomorrow, there would be presents for everyone. Santa would fly over the orphanage and Mary would wave him down. She'd been good this year, as had been the other children. Apart maybe from Brady, but it wasn't like he didn't have reason to be bad. It had taken his family 4 years to finally decide they didn't want him. Still, Mary couldn't help but feel a twinge of jealousy when she thought about it. He'd actually spent time with them.

Mary had asked Mother Superior if it was possible she remembered what her parents looked like. Her father had wavy brown hair, and her mother had blue eyes, she was sure of it. Mother Superior had said no. Her brain had been too young. But Mary swore she remembered. She shivered in the winter cold. It had begun to pierce through her cardigan.

Mary didn't dare admit it, but she hoped they would come back. But if they didn't, then a new teddy bear would be nice. Brady had taken hers. She let him have it. He could use the comfort. But if Santa thought she had been good enough, then maybe he'd let her see her family again. Just for a little while. She wanted to see her father's warm smile again. And her mother's blue eyes.

She wondered if they'd hold her tight, if they'd be proud of the girl she'd become. Deep down she hoped that if she was good enough, they'd want her. They'd regret leaving her at Saint Mary's and they'd ask for her forgiveness. And she'd say yes, and they'd be a family again.

A light shot across the sky, and Mary jumped up. It was Santa, she was sure of it. She shouted, and screamed for him to come down, but to no avail. Silence returned to the snow-covered gardens, and the sky was empty again. Mary sighed. Santa had forgotten them again. She sat down in the snow and stared up at the empty sky. Maybe it was her fault. Maybe if she made it to the top of the nice list, Santa wouldn't forget them. She'd just have to try harder next year.

Mary was lost in thoughts and plans and hadn't noticed the footsteps behind her, and jumped when a light touch ran across her hair. She turned, and joy shot up her spine. Her parents were here. After all this time, they had come for her, on Christmas morning. She threw her arms around them, but their touch was freezing. It bit into her but she held on ever tighter, whimpering in the cold. They were here, and they'd be together now. All was forgiven.

Dawn arose on Christmas day, and all the children arose from their beds but one. It was Mother Superior who had found her, cold as ice, arms tightly wound around a mound of snow, as the snowfall gently caressed her face.

12

THE COMFORT OF OUR LIVES

My beloved Marianne, I want to preface this by saying, as clearly as I can—I'm sorry. I've wrestled with these words, these thoughts for longer than anyone could possibly have imagined, and I don't think I've hidden it well. I pondered, my love, for the best part of a year, whether it would cause less pain for me to not even leave a note.

But I think that unanswered questions are their own form of agony, so here they are–my final words. If you're reading this, I'm already dead. I actually feel quite relieved. I don't know how to explain it. I've fallen in love with pain, and this death of mine is just me saying my vows, from the top of the Golden Gate Bridge.

Pain is so much more comforting than comfort, if you really think about it. I know. You're shocked to see me writing so eloquently. I haven't said much to you all in so many years, not since the heroin addled my mind. Well, the truth is, these words are old. I've been carrying them around for years, waiting for someone to read them. But what can I say? I feel the need to explain myself to you.

It started at Harvard. Law 203, Injury Law. I've relived that morning, time after time, as soon as the needle hit my veins, and my eyes rolled backwards into my skull. Felt the memory of the leather seats beneath my hand as the lecture replayed. *The Triangle Shirtwaist Factory Fire.* I memorized Mr. Taylor's words as soon as he said them.

The Comfort Of Our Lives

"Safety standards are written in blood. It's how we ensure tragedies never happen again."

His words echoed in my mind every time I saw so much as a fire hydrant. It was the beginning of my madness. The longer that class went on, the more I learnt, the less I could unsee. The codes that kept us safe, the decisions that saved our lives. I suppose it's a relief, isn't it, that no one's dying of asbestos anymore. But I can't help but feel this profound sense of loss.

I know, beloved. I sound as insane as ever. I'm here, about to kill myself because I miss industrial tragedies. Because I miss asbestos, fire exits that are kept locked, steamers that don't have enough lifeboats. From a certain perspective, I suppose that's true, and I imagine I look ridiculous, but you try it–there's no way to fall from a great height with dignity. The wind always finds a way to fuck up your hair.

No, I need you to understand, my darling– I was raised Catholic, while you were raised agnostic. The grace and the glory of God gave me all the purpose I needed to keep going. I think we all have something like that in our lives: work, the kids, the wife. Perhaps it's a mistake to put it all on black, so to speak. A diversified portfolio is more able to weather fluctuations, after all.

But God–God was everything to me. I loved him more than I loved myself, or indeed, you. I'm sorry, my love. I wish I'd loved you more. Perhaps we wouldn't be in this mess.

I believed He was good, and therefore I believed the world was good. But there is a fundamental reality I think we've grown accustomed to ignoring: life is not fit for human consumption. There's an old joke that goes "don't take life too seriously. None of us are making it out of here alive." I think it's important to remember.

You're raised Christian. So you believe in Eden Lost, in the punishment of the line of Eve. And yet, there is this understanding that we are God's favorite children. That creation is put here for us to enjoy. After all, we're special—we're the only creatures to have souls. The Christ perished on the cross for our sins. How could existence be anything less than ours?

There's a paradox, when it comes to God. I'm sure you've heard about it. There's no possibility to have a God who is all-powerful, all-knowing, and benevolent. It's a problem that's perplexed philosophers for very many years. But math was never my strong suit.

But enough dallying. Here it is, the horror of reality laid bare.

You will remember that I was struck by a car in my second year of law school. A hit and run. I was lying there, my dear, in a pool of my own blood soaking into the asphalt, listening to my own fading heartbeat. The cries of a million dying thoughts harmonizing into a choir of seraphim.

But all I could think of was how heavy these arms, these legs, this flesh... look! Even now Adenosine Triphosphate is firing, causing cells to writhe in agony as I wipe the tears from my face... I laid there my dear, still on the asphalt and heard the hum of existence. Hush now, my dear and listen—it starts with your heartbeat. That little trochaic pulse. Can you hear it, turning over like pistons in an engine? Now your mind. Those thoughts of yours. So loud in your mind.

Listen, my love! Do you hear them? Do you hear them vying for power, clamoring in your head, demanding their right to existence? Can you feel it, beloved? The fire in the air that molds itself to your thoughts, your fears, the heat of the forge of existence, the clamoring of the forge hammers, the rushing of the bellows...

Do you hear it, my adored? This is life. This is reality. Running in cycles. Every inanimate, conceptual thing, just as the vermin of the fields, vying for power, vying for the right to survive.

Don't you dare fight it. Please listen! The hum... there is no escaping it. It drove me mad, after the war, and I sought to dig it out from my head. I carved into my ears, silencing the world forever, and found that even the godforsaken silence sang to me in that broken melody, even the silence taunted me with the voices of dying angels, Marianne.

This is life. This is the curse of existence. Every moment, everything is rebuilding to carry on the illusion of life.

I sought the divine Marianne! I sought comfort in God, and when I got there, I saw the wrinkles on his face, as He too dissolved into nothing. There is no escape, Marianne. The hum sings for us all, Marianne. I found God, and all He had to offer me was tainted silence.

The EMTs arrived on the scene and found me sobbing. They believed it was from the pain, but the truth was it was from the truth: everything around us is dying. The hills are alive with the sound of screaming. And God? God was no different. He too was dying just as I was, in the cold of that hospital room, slowly pulling himself back together just to perish again. All that power, and he uses it merely to die, Marianne, over and over and over again.

Did you know that everyone has a pain tolerance beyond which their mind will go? Well not I. That ability was lost in the crash, was lost in the entourage of God. I felt it all, Marianne. They put me under, or at least they believed they did, and then I was brought under the knife.

I felt every laceration, Marianne. Every incision. Every suture. And Jove looked down on me with his pallid stare as I asked him, "Why? Why do you let me suffer?" Still he remained silent, and I watched the silence begin to die with him.

When I healed, I left for Sierra Leone. You will remember—I broke your heart, told you there was another woman. I'm sorry, Marianne. I knew not how else to tell you. I went out of fear and desperation. I had to know, Marianne. Did my Jehovah know?

I watched children die in mines so women could put

stones to their fingers. I watched men lose their limbs for their belief in freedom. The violence of insurgents against the women of the villages. And through all of it, I only had one question: "Jove, did you know?"

Still His face remained unspeaking.

I spent three years in Sierra Leone, until I could not take it any longer. I escaped in the night, tearing past the humanitarian relief tents, and took the first flight home.

The plane's droning hum burned itself into my ears. I watched a woman complain about her meal—I think they'd gotten her the wrong one—and I felt a deep revulsion from within the depths of my stomach. I unbuckled my seatbelt, walked across the aisle, and struck her, forcefully across the face. I got three years.

I still believe in the benevolence of God. Despite it all. Actually, I think it's us who have it all wrong

I spent three years in a cell, indulging in heroin. You know that much. But you do not know that I fell in love with it for its absence, and not its presence. You came to visit me once, to ask if there was any hope for us. I laughed in your face, and told you I had nothing to offer you but pain. That I would relish in scarring you, in destroying you, piece by piece. I offered you heroin, telling you that I wanted to watch the tracks run up your arm, caressing you with their touch.

You left then, and I do not blame you, my darling. But

understand, please, I was not repudiating you. It was my twisted holy declaration of love. Because something occurred to me, my darling. Jove, my beloved Jove, has adorned us with the gift of pain.

Pain. I have fallen in love with it, with the truth of reality. Everything around us is dying. Everything around us is screaming in pain. Pain is the foundation of reality. I have felt it since the day of the crash. Since I first saw the face of God. I know now the true name of God, and it is Pain.

We must not escape pain, escape suffering. We must embrace it, seek it, pursue it. It is the only thing that can capture the majestic boundlessness of God. It is the only thing that is freely available to us all. Hope is not. Joy is not. Love is not. But pain? Pain is so easy to obtain, and it is the end of all things.

My God is dissolving, fading away and releasing himself into the pain of decay. He will return soon to do it all again. And I? I'm standing atop the Golden Gate Bridge, and I cannot wait for the moment when my body will hit the water.

13
THE CICADA'S WHISPER

It was a scorching summer morn when Stephen arrived with a smug smile on his face and acne upon his brow. Others followed suit, readily exposing various features afforded to them by fickle fate: stubble marked chins descended in droves, accosted by the typical pubescent priory.

I had no interest for such things. At the time that my cohort had begun to consider the virtues of the opposite sex, I had managed to find a corner of the schoolyard away from the errant corrections of fate. There I made my residence, at least for the duration of recess.

My little lilac bush lay upon the grassy hill at the border of the asphalt court. It had grown awkward and misshapen, and so now shambled rather than stood. Its great branches surrounded an empty crawl space on all sides, and so, in the center of the leaves and pale purple flowers was a blanket I'd brought from home, and several small crates of comics.

It was an idyllic existence, that time between 11:00 and 12:30. The thick leaves insulated me from the incessant pounding of footballs against the schoolyard walls, and the incessant chatter of teenagers on their planned weekend conquests that never quite seemed to come to fruition.

After precisely two issues of Dennis The Menace, the school bells would release their ringing shriek, and haphazard lines would form, cleaving the courtyard into segments as I would emerge from my warm, soft cocoon, and join the disorder.

I will not hide it. I came to despise the lot of them, reeking as they did. I watched as they each reached that terrible age, *thirteen,* and prepared to count their maturity against the stubble on their chins and the blackheads on their nose.

Stephen had been the ninth of our cohort to undergo the process. I had watched as the pustulent sores took first Marcus, then Alton, then my friend John. And with their physical afflictions came a spiritual one. They wrapped their prior interests in boxes, trading them for the interests of the masses: football, cars, women.

I'd tried to bring my friend back to reality, inviting him around mine to read comics and play with action figures, and had earned a hard shove for my efforts.

"Get lost, baby," the impostor had ordered. "No one wants to play kid's games anymore."

He'd turned his back on me, and that was that. Eight years of friendship, ended with a mighty shove and leering at a poster of Claudine Auger.

The girls were no solace either. One by one they began coming to the schoolyard with shorter skirts, painted lips, fingernails, eyelids, as growths took root on their chests. Still I tried speaking to them, and found that we had little in common. Even Madeline, who I'd sometimes played House with, had little else to speak about other than the wonders of the pill.

I will admit, I began to fear for my life as I lived it. What would become of me on that horrible day? I was twelve and eleven months, and had come to regard my birthday with all the unease of a prisoner before the gallows.

I told my mother that I wished for there to be no affair at all, not even a little one. Just a normal day. She would not agree, but as June 18th fell on a Tuesday, and I had no one to invite, I got what I wanted in the end. She served me a chocolate cake in the morning, enough to spoil what little appetite had not been claimed by paranoia, and sent me on my way.

Screeches rippled across the courtyard that recess, just as waves ripple across a pond. An eerie whine cried from beneath my lilac tree and the unkept greens beside it. A sound like electric feedback, like static gone mad to the point of shrieking.

Cicadas. They'd hatched early from their thirteen-year slumber due to the unseasonal heat, mistaking June for August.

The ground crunched beneath our feet: the crisp, wet moistness of shattered exoskeleton. Wings shredded against the soles of boys' boots as they laughed. Empty red eyes stared out at the scene as the bugs accepted their fate. The boys ground them into a paste as I ran, eager to save my tree from the onslaught of these vermin.

My tree's branches enveloped me, but where the soft smell of flowers would once have greeted me, a putrid stench now assaulted my nostrils—the swarm had found my blankets, and several had mated until they died.

Rage overtook me, and grabbing a stone from off the ground, I began to beat at them, watching as my would-be blade cleaved a female in twain as she laid her eggs. I beat harder, beat more, felling a couple mid-coupling, and did not cease until the ground was littered with shattered chitin.

When I was certain I'd killed them all, I sat upon my blanket, panting. My weapon lay upon the ground, discarded. I traced my finger over the leaves of my beloved tree, but it was not the same as it once was. My wrath had left deep marks in its branches, and sap bubbled and poured from its wounds, dripping onto the ground below.

I wept, hemolymph smearing on my face as I wiped my tears. My sacred grove had been corrupted, twisted, and could never return to how it was again. Even my comics were stained with bug's insides. I would no longer have anywhere to hide from my adolescent cohort.

"I won't," I cried. "I won't join them! It will—It will grow back. I just—I just need to be patient."

My tree did not respond.

"Please!" I cried. "Please tell me you'll grow back!"

My tree remained silent, and I fell back into quiet sobs.

A rustling from beneath my blanket drew my attention, and I ceased my self-pitying. Drawing back my blanket, I watched as a cicada emerged from a tiny mound of dirt. I picked my stone from off the ground, and with a single blow, sent its head flying.

It landed upright upon my blanket, its beak trailing beneath its round red eyes. It stared at me as its body twitched, its legs filling the bush with those infernal clicks, "et tu, et tu, et tu," as it slowly died.

"Good riddance," I'd said, to no one in particular.

"Et tu," replied the cicada, one last time.

I sat there until the bell rang, mourning my childhood. I suppose now that it was all rather silly, but at the time it had felt like death. The bell had rung, and so I turned one last time to the warmth of the lilac branches, and thanked it for having sheltered me for so long. But I could deny my fate no more than the cicadas could deny theirs. For both of us, our thirteen years were up.

I gained my first protuberances that day: small jointed limbs, antenna, and a hard chitin shell. I joined the 7th graders as we lined up for algebra, and pondered if my dad might let me fix up his old Ford Mustang.

BRIGHTON
Independent Press

https://brightonindependentpress.co.uk/

First published in 2025 by Brighton Independent Press- Copyright © Petrichor Moss 2025

The right of Petrichor Moss to be identified as author of this work has been asserted in accordance with the Copyright, Designs and Patents Act 1988. All rights reserved. No part of this publication may be reproduced, stored in a retrieval system, or transmitted in photocopying, recording or otherwise, without the prior permission of the copyright owner.

This book is a work of fiction. Names, characters, businesses, organisations, places and events are either the product of the author's imagination or are used fictitiously. Any resemblance to actual persons, living or dead, events or locales is entirely coincidental.

ISBN: 978-1-917746-06-9

We hope you enjoyed this book...

... *and we hope to see you in the next one.*